My name is Antoinette Bergin. I have been a professional nanny for thirteen years during which time I have worked for over 142 families. No one seems to keep me on long. Which is okay. I came to America from London, England, and I've learned when Americans hire a British nanny they expect a certain stereotype. Actually, what they expect is British nanny movie quality perfection in the traditional sense. Apparently, this desired level of perfection is not what I bring to the table. This has led to many misunderstandings, hasty dismissals, and on one occasion involvement with local law enforcement.

I've since retired from the nanny business but the one aspect I truly miss is story telling. I love reading to children. Of course, I'm not pleased with fairy tales or any of the children's books I've researched. I believe them to be overly optimistic and stupid. I believe if you read overly optimistic and stupid stories to children, they will become overly optimistic and stupid people themselves. I prefer stories that entertain but at the same time prepare children for some of the realities waiting for them in the grown-up world.

Therefore, I write my own stories. 100% of parents that have heard my stories deem them wholly inappropriate for children.

Since I no longer nanny, I've compiled my stories into this book. I've called it "Bedtime Stories for Children You Hate" which may seem an odd title. However, looking back on my thirteen years, I did hate the children left in my charge. It was not their fault, really. They were born of parents with more money than brains and ideology that made utterly no practical sense. I was forbidden to read these stories to the children for which I cared and ironically, the lessons contained in them might have changed the little darlings into poppets I could tolerate.

I hope you read and enjoy my tales. Whether you share them with your children is entirely up to you. Even if you choose to keep the stories to yourself, I feel I've done something good here as most adults could also use a quick refresher course in unabridged reality.

Happy Reading and Best Wishes!
Antoinette

Table of Contents

Cover Art
By
Alex Phillips

Evie

Once upon a time in a land far... well, actually, it was just next door - there lived a girl named Evie. She was a sweet girl by all accounts. She did her homework before playing, brushed her teeth without being told, was kind to small animals, you know, basically just a good kid. If her mother said, "Chores?" Evie always responded with an eager, "Yes, please!"

I think at this point I've thoroughly illustrated that Evie was a chronically good child. Agreed? Good. Let's move on.

One morning as Evie walked to school (forty-five minutes early so she could organize the empty classroom into perfect symmetry as dictated by her OCD) she was approached by a tall man in a black trenchcoat. Evie's mother had educated her on this sort of fellow so immediately, Evie knew what to do.

She ran along the sidewalk (not in the street for we all know running in the street is only for bad girls) as fast as her tiny legs would take her. All the while she ran, she was appropriately yelling "Stranger Danger! Stranger Danger!" in her shrillest little girl voice. Of course, no one paid any mind to Evie because as a society we have all become quite detached and self-absorbed. We're all busy tweeting tweets, updating statuses, and other important things of that nature. Therefore, Evie's calls for help went unanswered. Still, she kept right on running with sweat dripping into her sweet little eyes causing her to experience severe vision impairment.

Sadly, Evie's eyesight became so compromised that the poor dear ran directly into the sturdy trunk of a 200 year old oak tree. Evie fell to the ground, completely unconscious. The tall man in the black trenchcoat sprinted to where helpless Evie had crumpled into a bloody, head wounded heap of a little girl type mess. Without a moment's hesitation he opened his ominous black satchel and performed emergency first aid with sterile gauze pads and hydrogen peroxide which he always carried with him as part of his natural disaster 72-hour preparedness kit.

The moral of the story should be apparent but in the event you weren't paying attention, I'll sum it up for you. The moral is this:

Not all tall men in black trenchcoats are sinister. Not all visually appealing, shade giving oak trees are nice. Lastly, I leave you with what I feel is the true lesson to be learned here. Even good girls, under the right circumstances, can wind up passed out on the ground in broad daylight with her skirt up over her head, and if one day perhaps you find your nanny in that precise condition, you might just want to give her explanation the benefit of the doubt rather than abruptly dismissing her, leaving her homeless and without references.

Will Fluffy Live Forever?

When I was a teenager I used to babysit a little girl named Beth. Beth had a cat she loved SO much. That cat and Beth were together day and night. One day Beth asked me, "Will Fluffy live forever?" I looked down into Beth's sweet, innocent blue eyes and knew the answer she was hoping to hear. Instead, I told her the truth.

"Oh, God, no!" I replied. "Not only will Fluffy not live forever, since you let her outside all the time, she'll probably die soon."

Beth's eyes welled up with tears and she hugged Fluffy tight against her. "What do you mean?" implored Beth, hoping I would explain how Fluffy was somehow exempt from this awful rule of nature. I decided I would tell her the story of Sam. Sam was a gray striped cat that wandered into our back yard when I was a little girl and we kind of just kept her. We eventually figured out Sam was female, which made Sam short for Samantha. The reason we didn't know Sam's gender sooner was because my parents wouldn't pick Sam up to examine her genitals and when I looked, I had no idea what I was looking for. The way we stumbled onto Sam's womanhood was that she became pregnant. You see, my parents were farm folk. They saw veterinary care for pets as frivolous and ridiculous. Cats were for mice catching and if you happened to love them as well, that was fine, as long as you recognized that cats died. Be it from illness or accident, cats died and there would be no sentimental intervention. There would be no costly spaying, neutering or vaccinating because a cat was a cat and all of the aforementioned precautions were rubbish invented by city folk who loved to waste money.

Sam's belly began to hang low and she had nipples popping out all over her undercarriage. That's when Dad declared in his simple wisdom, "I suppose Sam is a girl." I was so excited at the prospect of having Sam's kittens join the family. I couldn't wait! Then one day Sam started yowling in agony. It didn't seem she had been pregnant for very long. Could she possibly be having her litter already? I prepared a soft, secluded bed for Sam with my doll blankets and encouraged her to lie down. She didn't want to. Instead, she walked slowly around the back yard in circles wailing a horrid noise. I sat behind the storage shed with my knees pulled up to my chest and sobbed. I was of no use to Sam and I felt ashamed and helpless. I vowed to make it up to her when her babies were born. I'd take such good care of them all!

After several hours, Sam finally quieted and settled into the doll blanket bed. She was exhausted. I comforted her and tried to give her water but she only wanted sleep. While Sam slept, I set out to find where she had left her kittens. Surely, they needed looking after. I scoured the back yard looking for a nook or cranny where Sam may have given birth. In the wide open area of the lawn I found a tiny, fleshy blob. I picked it up and realized to my horror it was an underdeveloped cat fetus. It had the beginnings of paws and facial features and a miniscule tail. It was also quite dead. I ran to my father screaming and crying. "Daddy! Help me, please! Look what I've found!"

Mother came outside to investigate the ruckus and saw what I cradled in my hands. She ran into the kitchen and came back with a paper towel. She snatched the kitten fetus from me with the towelette, threw it in the waste bin and dragged me to the loo to scrub my hands clean. She explained to me that Sam had miscarried her litter and there would be no living babies. She told me not to be sad because we still had Sam. Dad appeared in the hallway and asked, "Is that the only one you found?" I nodded. He rubbed his chin with his hand for a moment while he thought. "There's bound to be more," he said flatly. "Damn. I really don't want those things mucking up the lawn mower."

The next thing I knew I was combing the back lawn like a one person search party with a plastic sack in one hand and a work glove on the other. I spent that Summer afternoon plucking kitten fetuses out of the grass. There were eight. Actually, nine. I missed one and it did muck up the lawn mower.

I worried Sam would become pregnant again and we'd have a repeat of that nasty day. As it turned out, I worried in vain. Later that same week, Sam went frolicking in the field behind our house. She never came home. My brother took pity on my dreadful mental state and went looking for her. He came home empty handed. He said Sam was dead in the field. Apparently run down by a tractor. He tried to retrieve her body for proper burial but the villainous farmer that owned the field had opened fire on my brother with a pellet gun. The old bastard shot salt bits at anyone he caught on his property.

I hoped Beth had learned from my cautionary tale and would try to keep Fluffy in the house as much as possible. It was then I noticed Beth and Fluffy were gone. I'd been talking to myself for God knows how long. Beth was throwing up in the bushes while Fluffy watched attentively.

I was never asked to look after Beth again. I suppose she'd just gotten too old for a sitter.

Your Upstairs Neighbor Kills People

Andy's palms were sweaty and the phone kept slipping as he tried to call Claire. Andy and Claire had been friends practically since birth. They lived next door to each other until they were twelve. The year Andy and Claire turned twelve, it was discovered that Andy's mum was sleeping with Claire's dad. It was a particularly upsetting discovery because it happened during Andy's birthday party. The usually discreet adulterous couple were spotted in the wine cellar by the magician hired to amaze the children. Apparently, Bob the Magnificent found it much easier to be amazing after a few swigs of cheap vodka. He figured no one would be fetching wine from the cellar during a kid party, so he slipped in quietly and found Claire's dad also slipping into something albeit not so quietly. That something, obviously, was Andy's mum. The whole incident could have been swept under the rug for a nominal fee collected by Bob, but there was no reasonable lie that could explain why Andy's mum had her cleavage full of birthday cake frosting and why Claire's dad's tongue was blue.

Now, two years later, Andy and his mum lived in a flat on the other side of town. Andy remained close friends with Claire because they were a mere bike ride apart and after Andy's twelfth birthday party, they surprisingly felt closer than ever. They had decided that all the illicit parent swapping that had taken place made them honorary siblings.

Andy finally got Claire on the phone. "Claire... You've got to come over," Andy pleaded desperately. Claire had heard this tone many times before. She sighed.

"Andy, come on. I'm busy. I've got a ton of homework."

"Pleeaasse," nagged Andy. "Do your homework here. You know I can't be alone," he paused for emphasis then said in a deep, throaty voice, "and you know why." Claire knew she could spend the next twenty minutes arguing and it wouldn't make a bit of difference. She'd end up at Andy's no matter what. She grabbed her knapsack and in no time she stood poised to knock on Andy's front door. Before she had the chance, Andy flung it open, grabbed Claire's wrist and yanked her into the foyer. He slammed the door shut and locked it extra hard as if turning the bolt extra hard would let the lock know he was serious.

"Thanks for coming," said Andy quite pathetically.

Claire stood rigid and said, "Andy, I am here once and for all to convince you that..."

Andy cut her off mid-sentence. "No," he said. "This time, I'll convince you."

Claire rolled her eyes and flopped down on the sofa. "You will never convince me that your upstairs neighbor kills people."

"I will," Andy said firmly. "This time I have a plan to

acquire irrefutable evidence that my upstairs neighbor does, in fact, kill people."

"It's going to be a long night, isn't it?" moaned Claire.

"Perhaps," said Andy, "but one you'll never forget."

When it started to get dusky outside, Andy decided it was time to order take away. He knew a Chinese restaurant in the neighborhood that delivered. Claire complained. "You know I don't like Chinese food."

"Good," said Andy, "because it's not for you." Claire grew visibly irritated.

"What - you're just going to eat in front of me? I'm starving, you prick!"

"It's not for me either," barked Andy. "It's for the upstairs neighbor."

"So, I'm starving, you force me to come over here, then you reward your alleged serial killer neighbor with free food. Oh. That takes the cake, Andy."

"Funny you should mention cake," mumbled Andy.

"What was that?" asked Claire.

Andy ignored the question and said, "Hush yourself. I've got to concentrate."

"Right. I'll be in the kitchen foraging for supper," Claire

said as she headed down the hallway leaving Andy with his eye pressed intently against the peephole in the door. He wanted to know the precise moment the Chinese delivery man arrived.

About an hour passed and Claire was working on her mathematics homework when Andy yelled, "He's here! He's going up the stairs!" He grabbed his jacket from the coat rack and instructed Claire to be the lookout.

"What am I looking out for, Andy?" she asked and slammed her text shut.

"I'm going to catch my upstairs neighbor in the act of murder!" he squealed as he ran outside. "If I'm not back in five minutes, call the police!"

"Andy, don't be stupid!" she yelled, but he was already gone. She stared at her wristwatch until five minutes had passed. She heard no sound from above and she certainly wasn't going to play the fool and call the police. She ran up the stairs to the flat above Andy's and simply rang the bell. No one answered. Not knowing what to do, she tried the doorknob. It wasn't locked. She carefully opened the door just a bit and called "Hello!" into the dark room.

She heard Andy's voice whisper, "Help me, Claire!"

Claire then pushed the door fully open and barged into the room and screamed, "Don't you dare hurt Andy!" She heard a sort of crinkling sound behind her which made her spin around. Whomp! Was the next sound she heard which was a plastic rubbish bag being yanked over her head and fastened around her neck.

Claire must have lost consciousness because the next thing she remembered was awakening tied to a wooden chair. The bag had been removed from her head and the lights had been turned on. Before her stood Andy and a Chinese man. From the looks of things, the two of them had been feasting on orange chicken and fried rice while they waited for her to come to. Claire was beyond confused. "Andy?" She asked with puzzlement. "What..." Her voice trailed off.

Andy replied, "Where are my manners? Claire, meet my upstairs neighbor, Chanming Chin. He kills people."

Claire tried to speak but she didn't know what to say. Andy waved a springroll around in his hand while he regaled Claire with his self-proclaimed brilliance. "I told you my upstairs neighbor killed people but as usual, you didn't listen. You never listen to me. Well, listen now.

Your randy father fucked up my twelfth birthday by fucking my mother which consequently fucked up my life." Andy bit viciously into the springroll, tearing it angrily with his teeth. "Your parents reconciled which was lovely for you, but mine didn't! NOT MINE!" Andy yelled in a crazy voice Claire had never heard before. "Your life went on as usual and Mum and me had to move into this shit flat after Dad divorced her and to top it off, we live under a man who kills people!"

Claire stammered but finally eeked out some words. "None of that's my fault, Andy," she said as she sobbed. "You're so angry at me that you've befriended a serial killer? I don't understand!"

"That's so typical of you, Claire. You still can't see past your own theories and assumptions and make room for the possibility you may not be correct." Andy was right in her face now and as he spoke, bits of cabbage shot from his mouth onto her face. "I never said my upstairs neighbor was a serial killer. That was your conclusion. I never said serial killer. I said he kills people. He's a hitman, you daft bitch. I've hired him to kill you. I've been saving for two years. It would've taken forever but my mum figured it all out and took on an extra job to pitch in. Your parents are dead right now in the basement of the beautiful house you didn't have to move out of. Next week you'll be mourned by classmates at the school you never had to leave. Mum and I will be in Brazil with Chanming Chin."

Chanming Chin stood as if he had been given his cue and choked the life right out of Claire's body, effectively ending Andy and Claire's lifelong friendship. Before Andy had time to gloat or regret or even burp, Chanming Chin choked the life right out of Andy's body, effectively ending Andy's mum's fourteen year run as a mother. Andy's mum emerged from the bedroom closet with a packed suitcase and before Andy's mum had time to gloat or regret or even shed a tear, Chanming Chin choked the life right out of her body.

Chanming Chin looked around the room at the carnage. He removed the airline tickets to Brazil from Andy's mum's dead fingers. Chanming Chin was, in fact, a serial killer. He'd just never gotten paid for it before.

As Chanming Chin boarded the plane for Brazil with his longtime boyfriend, Bob the Magnificent, he felt like the luckiest Chinese homosexual serial killer in the world.

Kevin's First (And Last) Trip to the Zoo

At long last endless winter gave way
To sunshine on a warm Springtime day.

Little Kevin, hair blond, eyes blue,
Begged his mum for a trip to the zoo.

"I'm big now, Mum," Kevin implored.
"I'll behave all day and not get bored!"

Kevin's mum paused for a moment to think.
"You were booted out of the ice skating rink."

"That was ages ago and not quite fair,
It was never proven I touched Mindy *there*."

Mum shook her head. She wasn't convinced.
She remembered the circus, clutched her forehead and winced.

"Oh, Mum! At the circus I was merely a kid.
Besides, I barely recall what you think that I did."

"Elephant stampede," Mum replied straight away.
Peanuts, a slingshot, a clown trampled in hay."

"I promise you, Mum. This is now. That was then.
I've not been to the zoo and I'm already ten!"

"Alright," Mum relented but she still had her doubts.
"You cause me one fig of trouble, Mister, we're on the outs."

"I'll punish you harshly, like you'll never believe!"
"Fear not, dear Mum. I've nothing up my sleeve."

They arrived at the zoo. Kevin was delighted!
Mum even felt good that her boy was excited.

An hour flew by as they had such good fun.
Mum let her guard down which she shouldn't have done.

She stood in a queue to buy Kev a sno-cone.
For a slice of an instant, that left him on his own.

By the time Mum had paid and had sno-cone in hand,
The landscape had changed on a scale that was grand.

The giraffes were on fire, the zebras ran free.
A monkey waged war from the top of a tree.

It swung by its tail while flinging its poo
At the crowd down below who knew not what to do.

The kiddy train derailed, peacocks ran amok.
Penguins were beating on an innocent duck.

Brown bears and lions tore each other to shreds.
Snakes crawled on hippos mercilessly biting their heads.

The scene was horrific, the stench even worse.
A woman fought parrots by flailing her purse.

Evacuation techniques weren't working as planned.
Too much staff had been eaten. The zoo was largely
unmanned.

Mum was swept towards an exit, Kevin nowhere in sight.
She felt certain he'd caused this. He'd never been right.

Mum ambled through the car park staring blankly ahead.
She worried and wondered if her Kevin was dead.

She'd wait by the auto for as long as it took
To claim Kevin's body but wait... have a look.

Asleep in the car on the seat in the rear
Was Kevin curled up looking really quite dear.

Mum drove them home, her mind filled with confusion.
She knew, like before, she'd reach no conclusion.

Was Kevin to blame or was it maybe by chance?
Was her young son a demon or was it all happenstance?

She'd continue to wonder but one thing she knew.
Never again would they go to the zoo.

I Said Not to Touch That

David, a bright and inquisitive boy, had one favorite question which he asked incessantly. "What's that?" he asked. He asked it all the time about everything. He asked it even when you could be fairly certain he already knew what an object was. He asked it until you wanted to punch him in the face. Really hard.

As David's nanny, I had one steadfast rule. Do not enter my personal bedroom when I'm not on duty. Further, do not enter my personal bedroom when I am on duty. If you are saying to yourself right now, "I believe that is two rules," you are wrong. It is one rule with a clarification. Do not enter my personal bedroom when I am not on duty because I am probably in there and I don't want to see you if I'm not being paid to do so. Further, and this is the clarification, do not enter my personal bedroom when I am on duty because I will never be in there. If I am not in there but you are, it can only be because you're a nosy little bastard.

So life with David went pretty much like this: "David, do you want a scrambled egg for breakfast?"

"What's that?" David would ask in a nasally tone of voice, smashing the two words together into more of a sound than the English language. "S'tha?" he seemed to be saying.

"A scrambled egg, David, as you well know, is what you had for breakfast yesterday and the day before that and also the day before that and so on and so on until we have back-traced an approximate month of scrambled eggs."

"Poached," replied David.

"Fine. Poached it is," I'd say, knowing full well we would have the same conversation each morning from now on for an approximate month with just the word "poached" substituted for the word "scrambled."

I was required to take David for a walk through the countryside every day. I think his mother feared he would become a fat fuck like his father lest we stick to the daily wilderness outing routine. David's constant query "What's that?" (or "S'tha?" if you recall) forced me into the habit of always answering, "That is a (fill in the blank). Don't touch it." "Don't touch it" became my incessant answer because David would inevitably ask about the most disgusting or dangerous item he could find. I am of the opinion that he liked to make me explain icky and stupid concepts.

For example, "S'tha?" would blurt David as he pointed at the ground.

"That is an old dried up cow pie. Don't touch it." I'd say.

"S'tha?"

"That is a poisonous mushroom. Don't touch it."

"S'tha?"

"That is a dead bird carcass. Don't touch it."

"S'tha?"

"That is an evil lizard creature. Don't touch it."

I don't know why I even bothered to say "Don't touch it" as David would always, without exception, immediately touch it.

God, I hated David. I prayed every morning for the inner serenity I needed to prevent his untimely, yet completely understandable, death. You see, in addition to the tedious "S'tha?", David continually violated my very clear policy of keep your body, and for that matter, your voice, away from my personal bedroom at all times. On my night off David would come to my room in the basement. A closed door meant nothing to David (a trait he undoubtedly learned from his fat fuck father who repeatedly committed the same "accidental faux pas" with my bedroom door).

"S'tha?" David would ask and point.

"That is my left breast. It has apparently popped out of my nighty. Don't touch it."

"S'tha?"

"That is my clenched fist. It's about to touch you."

The threat of physical harm sent David running but that was only a temporary solution. I needed to really drive home how serious I was about my one and only rule. I'd need to prepare and execute a plan on my fucking day off.

It really didn't take long to set the components in order. I'd chosen a very basic premise to teach David the lesson he needed to learn. An entire week later on my next night off, David flung open my personal bedroom door and straight away spotted the shiny new object I had prominently displayed just for him. "S'tha?" David yelled with a bit of extra enthusiasm at the unexpected thrill of seeing something that he genuinely did not recognize.

"That is a fully activated, spring loaded, sharp-toothed, reinforced iron bear trap. Don't touch it," I said firmly. Of course, David touched it.

I think David's lesson was well learned. He eventually adapted to life with one arm. Children are very resilient. Despite the fact that I lost my job, had to leave the country and live under an assumed name for many years, my only regret is that I didn't have the opportunity to reset the lesson for David's fat fuck father. I did, however, leave detailed instructions tucked between the mattresses of my personal bedroom's bed for my successor. I felt it was the least I could do for a fellow nanny.

First Love

Even though Kelly was a full three years older than Kate, they were as close as two sisters could be. They shared secrets, clothes and a solid stick antipersperant/deodorant. They did not share a bedroom but they may as well have. Whatever room Kelly occupied, one was sure to find Kate, and vice versa.

On Friday, the 21st of January, Kate bestowed upon Kelly the secret she had been longing to possess ever since the girls' mother first read them a series of truly ridiculous fairy tales. Kate was in love for the very first time. "Oh, Kate!" remarked Kelly with genuine glee. "You must tell me in full and don't dare skip a detail!" Kate blushed and giggled, which caused Kelly to blush and giggle. They grabbed at one another's hands until their fingers somehow managed to clasp and squeeze. The girls stood face to face, hands in a tangle, blushing and giggling and, of course, the only logical thing to do next was to begin jumping up and down together in unison. This behavior continued for a good nineteen minutes and resulted in Kelly and Kate both dropping to the floor unconscious due to lack of oxygen.

The sisters awoke on the hardwood floor approximately thirty-seven minutes later, dizzy and confused, with a couple of visible bruises and a bump on the noggin. Luckily (for Kate, anyway) Kelly had broken her sister's fall with her own body so just the one head was harmed.

(Note from the Author: Now do you see the damage done to children by those fucking fairy tales?)

Upon sorting themselves out, Kelly and Kate decided to resume any further discussions of love while resting on the safety of Kelly's pillow-top mattress. "He's positively dreamy," gushed Kate.

"Who is it?" demanded Kelly in impatient fashion.

"Ronald Lockheed," whispered Kate with a purposely sly glance in Kelly's direction.

Kelly bolted upright on the bed. "Did you just say Ronald Lockheed?" she asked incredulously.

Kate propped herself up on her elbows and asked, "What's the matter with Ronald Lockheed?"

"Well, nothing in particular," said Kelly. "It's just that you've known Ronnie since you were five. You've never made note of said 'dreaminess' before. What's changed?"

"First of all," answered Kate, "he no longer prefers to be called Ronnie. Please refer to him as Ronald which is his proper name." Kate continued with her second point. "Ronald's father just came into an unbelievable amount of money from some kind of business deal. Ronald paid me a handsome sum just to walk through Downington Park with him." Kelly stared at her little sister in horror. Words failed her and she sat fixed in position which Kate took as a sign to carry on with the story. "Then just yesterday," Kate said while absent-mindedly inspecting her fingernails, "Ronald bought me a chocolate bar, a package of Jammie Dodgers, and this necklace." With her thumb and index finger she pulled out a small silver chain that had been tucked away underneath her sweater. She now dangled it for Kelly to admire. Kelly leaned in to inspect it closer.

"Is that a real diamond?" she asked in such a high pitched tone that she came close to a frequency only dogs could hear.

"No," Kate replied casually. "It's a cubic zirconia which is practically as good."

Kelly scoffed. "It's not practically as good. He probably purchased it from a street vendor for the price of bubble gum."

"You're jealous!" Kate squealed with unmistakable joy.

"I am not!" Kelly defended. "Jealous of an itty bitty cubic zirconia given to you by Ronnie 'I always have a runny nose' Lockheed? Don't be daft."

Kate laughed. "Jealous! Jealous!" she sang to antagonize Kelly. Kelly hopped off the bed and stood with her hands angrily on her hips.

"Kate," she said, sounding an awfully lot like their mother, "I regret to inform you that your acceptance of these gifts is in questionable taste."

"What does that mean?" responded Kate who had taken an equally defensive position with her body.

"It means, dear sister, you are beginning to sound like a whore! Do you even like Ronnie?" Surprisingly, that question didn't make Kate angry.

"Not really," she admitted. Kelly slapped her hand to her forehead in disbelief.

"Whore!" she yelled loudly at her baby sister, who no longer seemed babyish at all.

"Take that back!" screamed Kate.

"I will not!" shouted Kelly.

"Then I'm going to my own room, shutting the door and pretending I'm an only child," Kate announced haughtily then left Kelly's room, slamming the door as if it were an exclamation point.

The previously inseparable sisters were now not even acknowledging the other's existence. Their mother was thoroughly confused but since neither sister would offer an explanation, she decided to let them work it out amongst themselves. It wasn't until Saturday, the 12th of February, that Kate finally walked silently into Kelly's bedroom. Her head was bowed as if she were studying her shoes. Kelly ignored her sister for as long as she could stand before her curiosity got the better of her. She set aside the book she'd been reading and asked Kate matter of factly, "What do you want?"

"Nothing," Kate said quietly. "I just thought you should know that Ronnie, I mean Ronald," she said mockingly, "dumped me today." Kelly could see her little sister was hurt and confused but still, on principle, she wasn't going to be a sympathetic shoulder to cry on just yet.

"Why?" asked Kelly. "Did he figure out you were using him for his money?"

"Not exactly," said Kate as she plopped into a chair near her sister. "Apparently, Ronnie was using me."

"How so?" asked Kelly, now actually caring a bit about her sister's obvious pain. Kate began to cry.

"He said he was practicing with me and that he thought I knew because we'd known each other since we were five."

"Practicing what?" asked Kelly, who at this point had been drawn back into big sister mode.

"Practicing being a boyfriend," sighed Kate, her embarrassment showing through. "You see, he plans to approach Gemma Breckenthorpe on Valentine's Day and attempt to win her affections with an elaborate display of gentlemanly manners and expensive gifts including a real diamond necklace."

Kelly needed a moment to work this out in her head. "So, he practiced being a boyfriend on you so he could win over the town trollop?"

"Yep." said Kate. Kelly erupted in laughter. Kate failed to see the humor of the situation. Kelly hugged Kate and kneeled down beside her.

"Katie Pie," said Kelly sweetly, "there are so many ways to explain what happened here that I can't decide which one to go with."

"I want to know them all," Kate replied angrily.

"Alright," sighed Kelly as she prepared a tutorial in her head. "One explanation is that Ronnie's an idiot. Gemma's dad is an abusive alcoholic. That's why Gemma's such a slut. She'll put out for any boy who offers her a kind word. Ronnie's grand theatrics will be totally lost on her." Kate listened with intensity to Kelly's every wise word.

"Another explanation is that you got played but you don't really deserve any compassion because you thought you were playing Ronnie. Therefore, one might say the player justly got played."

Kate reluctantly nodded. "You're right. I never even liked Ronnie. I just felt stupid when he dumped me."

"Did you get to keep all your gifts?" asked Kelly.

"Well, yeah," answered Kate.

"Well then you didn't come out too badly," Kelly explained using somewhat complicated hand gestures to try to keep everyone correctly categorized. "You, as the player, got what you were playing for. So on that point, you win. However, you were also an unknowing and foolish playee. For that, you lose a pride point, but your heart hasn't been broken so you'll have a quick recovery." Kate was mesmerized by her sister's vast knowledge. "So then next," Kelly considered briefly, "we could go into the concept of good and bad karma, but frankly, I think I could sum it up quickly by saying as of now, you and Ronnie both have terrible trouble with karma." Kate nodded again and looked as though more tears might be coming so Kelly quickly added, "But karma is easy to repair. Say seven 'Hail Marys' and eleven 'Our Fathers'."

"Isn't that Catholic stuff?" asked Kate. "I don't know how to do those things you just said. We're Church of England."

"Right. I know," said Kelly, "but I saw it on the telly and I thought it sounded neat." Kate rolled her eyes. "Okay, I'll be serious now," Kelly assured. "Just do random acts of kindness for about a week and then stop being such a prat."

"Will do," promised Kate as she got up to head for the kitchen.

"Oh, wait," called Kelly. "I heard something else on the telly. It went like this: Don't hate the game, hate the players. I think. Or maybe it was hate the game instead of the players. That doesn't sound right either." Kelly had her eyes closed, and was mumbling to herself while waving her hand around as if she were trying to map out a saying that made sense.

"Kelly," said Kate completely destroying her sister's imaginary blueprint. Kelly opened her eyes and looked at Kate. "I've come up with a saying of my own that ought to cover it all."

"Let's hear it," Kelly said eagerly. Kate stiffly straightened her posture and decreed, "Hate the game, hate the players, hate the played, hate the town slut, hate everything."

"Oh, that's quite good," Kelly said as she grabbed a pen from her desk. "Let's write that down."

"Fine," said Kate, "as long as we go for ice cream afterward."

"Deal!" cried Kelly, and just like that, everything returned to normal between the sisters.

"Thank God!" said the girls' mother after they were out of earshot. "I was running out of liquor." Mother filled a glass with the very last of the scotch and settled herself on the sofa. She didn't even notice her cherished heirloom book of fairy tales burning in the fireplace.

Pretty, Pretty Petal

A beautiful rose bloomed on the bush nearest the cottage's front porch. It was a magnificent and perfect blend of red and pink, with just the slightest hint of orange on the outer edge. Reggie had watched it grow from a tiny bud into a stunning blossom. He wanted to take a photograph of it but he didn't have a camera. He lost his on the family's last trip to the seaside and hadn't yet saved enough money to buy a new one. He thought perhaps he could paint its portrait but alas, the lad had no artistic talent. Reggie leaned over the porch's wooden railing several times per day to inhale the sweet and robust fragrance of the flawless flower with which he had become obsessed.

One evening as Reggie was preparing for bed he was overcome with the desire to be near his precious rose. He crept quietly out of the house and onto the porch. Oh, how he yearned to snip that stem and claim the rose all for himself. He resisted the urge knowing that the rose would die much faster in a vase as opposed to being left in its natural abode. "Maybe just a petal," he thought. "Surely the rose won't miss one pretty, pretty petal. After all, it has so many." He'd carefully pluck a single petal from the outside layer of the rose. "It won't matter," Reggie consoled himself, "I'll take it from the side of the rose which is partially concealed by the other stems and leaves." As delicately as possible, Reggie removed the chosen petal with surgeon-like precision. He trembled with satisfaction as he felt the petal's velvety smoothness against his hand. He inspected the rose thoroughly. "It doesn't show a bit!" he whispered as he tip-toed back into the cottage and to his bedroom. He filled a shallow crystal dish with cool water and in it he floated his pretty, pretty petal. With the dish next to his bed he felt he'd sleep well and his petal would be the first thing to greet him when he awoke.

Reggie was on the verge of nodding off when he thought he heard someone speak. "Hello..." he said quietly and waited for a reply. He heard nothing.

Just as his head was about to make contact with his pillow he clearly heard the words "I miss my mummy."

"What?" said Reggie but he had no idea with whom he was speaking.

"I miss my mummy. Why did you take me?" Reggie was terrified. He'd never given much thought to whether or not ghosts existed but he had nothing by way of explanation as to this small, soft voice. A voice that could be described as... oh, dear God! No! The voice was *velvety*! Reggie allowed his eyes to move just a bit to the dish where his pretty, pretty petal floated in the now lukewarm water. "Why did you take me?" asked the petal. Reggie gasped in horror not only because a rose petal was speaking to him, but also because at that moment he realized the seriousness of what he had done!

Reggie bent down close to the dish and said to the petal,

"I'm so sorry little petal," he apologized. "What can I do to make this right?"

"Nothing," the petal answered sadly. "You've killed me. The life is slowly leaving me as we speak." Reggie began to cry but the petal kept speaking. "I hurt," it said. "I hurt around my bottom where you tore me from my mummy." Reggie was weeping something awful by now but still, the petal spoke. "I know my mummy must be hurting, too. She's got nothing but a jagged vacancy where you stole me from her." Reggie was now out of bed, kneeling on the floor, begging the petal for forgiveness. "I have none to give you," said the petal. "I will never forgive you, my mummy will never forgive you, and none of my aching brothers or sisters will forgive you. By morning, I, and my entire family shall be dead and it's all your fault."

"No, please!" begged Reggie. "There must be something I can do to correct my wrongdoing!" but the petal had gone silent. It had spoken its last words. The pretty, pretty petal was dead. Reggie clawed his face with his own hands and moaned, "I'm a murderer. I've killed the one thing in life I ever loved and it died a horrible death! Alone and separated from its family by just a few heartbreaking meters!" Reggie's racing thoughts quickly turned to the rest of the flower. He flung open the cottage door and ran to the wooden railing of the porch. He bent over so quickly, without any concern for his safety, that he almost launched himself into the yard. His face was closer to the rose than it had ever been before and he beseeched it to speak to him. The rose remained mute. "Oh, God!" Reggie wailed as his body fell listlessly onto the old, creaky wood of the porch. "I am the master of death. As long as I walk this earth there shall be no beauty."

Morning came bringing with it the delivery of that day's newspaper. The paper boy, twelve year old Charles Mapleby, received the shock of his young life. From a beam in the porch's rafters hung fifty-nine year old Reginald Halford. Pale and dead from a self-inflicted broken neck.

Officials were called and neighbors gathered in the street. An emergency worker on a ladder cut through the rope to free Reggie from his status as a human piñata. His body was lowered onto a stretcher and hauled away while the neighbors loitered outside in their housecoats, hair curlers, bathrobes and slippers. "I can't believe he finally did it," said old Mr. Jensen, who hadn't had time to insert his dentures. Mrs. Jensen dropped to her knees on the pavement and began to pray for Reggie's soul.

"I suppose it was just a matter of time," stated Mrs. Albertson.

"I heard he stopped taking his meds months ago," said Mr. Jarvis, at which point, Mr. Cooper, the local pharmacist, turned red in the face and said, "I told you that in confidence, Richard!"

"Well, I suppose, gentlemen, there's no use getting worked up over old Reggie's privacy now," said Mrs. Sheets, who was known about town for her sense of logical reasoning. "I further suggest," said Mrs. Sheets, "that we congregate at someone's home for morning tea rather than stand out of doors in our underclothes." There were murmurs of agreement which seemed unanimous so the residents of Rockypath Lane headed to Jean Remford's house because everyone knew she had the largest dining room. God knows she reminded them of that fact whenever an occasion arose for assembly.

That was the last anyone ever spoke of Mr. Reginald Halford who once grew the most beautiful roses in all of Bremmington Township.

I Thought We Were Camping

Nigel and his mum, Marianne, were having a wonderful Summer. Marianne had taken a great long holiday from work and much to Nigel's liking, the pair were spending the entire Summer camping. Nigel loved to camp and fish and hike and collect rocks and anything else he could think of even remotely related to the act of camping. It surprised him quite a bit that his mum had decided to take him camping, especially for three whole months, because Marianne was not much of an outdoor person. She tolerated camping before Nigel's father had died, but never really seemed to enjoy it. Perhaps she was finally coming out of her grief over her husband's death, but whatever the reason, Nigel was simply happy to be in the woods.

Marianne suggested that they play a game. Nigel was always up for a good game. What Marianne proposed was that she and Nigel pretend to be wilderness experts and try to live off the land without delving into their store bought supplies. To Nigel, this was the greatest, most adventurous thing his mum had ever even thought of, let alone wanted to play. "Absolutely, Mum!" said Nigel with great enthusiasm. They had begun playing the game over two months ago and had only twice found it necessary to open a can of beans or soup if they failed to catch anything for dinner. It was slow going at first, but as their fishing and foraging skills improved, they had virtually all of their non perishable items still successfully packed away in a crate.

Nigel was proud of Marianne. He'd never seen this side of her before. He had no idea his Mum was a nature girl at heart.

As the days passed, Nigel often found himself dreading going home at the Summer's end. He loved living the life of a huntsman, fisherman, woodsman and any other title he could think up to bestow on himself. Time passed quickly, as it does when you are enjoying yourself. Eventually, the other campers started leaving and new ones stopped taking their place. Nigel couldn't believe Marianne's power of endurance. He thought surely she would have forced him to go home long before now, but she seemed to be having as much fun as he. Sometimes he thought he saw Marianne crying which confused him. Marianne explained she wasn't really crying because they were tears of happiness. She was grateful that she had such a good son in Nigel and told him this had been one of the best Summers of her life. The only thing that would have made it perfect, she said, was if Nigel's father could have been here to enjoy it as well.

Finally, all the other campers had gone home but, strangely, Marianne seemed steadfast in her resolve to stay. She told Nigel she was very fond of the woodland home they had created with a lovely tent and new amenities as often as their imaginations and found materials would allow. Then, without prior notice, Marianne made a proposal which not only amazed Nigel, but also transformed him into the happiest boy on the planet. Marianne said she had been thinking a lot during the night while Nigel slept. She said there was an awful lot to be learned at his age that couldn't be taught from books. Rather, there were some lessons one could only learn though experience. As for the educational content that could be extracted from texts, Marianne had inside her head. She was a very smart woman who had a job that required her to teach employees under her charge lots of things all the time. She said she could practically be considered a teacher of sorts.

Nigel couldn't believe what he thought Marianne was saying but to his astonishment, she was saying exactly what he thought. She wanted to continue this experiment of sorts through the Fall, Winter, Spring and even into the next Summer if she could manage so much time away from work. Nigel thought he would burst with pure joy!

"Great!" exclaimed Marianne. "Why don't you stay here and start the fire for dinner while I make sure our plan is approved by the Park Ranger."

"Okay, Mum!" beamed Nigel. He didn't know what had come over her, but he loved his mum more than ever. He smiled, took a deep breath of the fresh pine scented air and got to work on the fire.

Meanwhile, Marianne hiked down the trail to the Ranger Station. "Hello, Marianne!" yelled Ranger Frederick from a distance as he waved his arm wildly in an overly friendly gesture.

Marianne waved back in the same overblown manner and reciprocated, "Hello, Ranger Frederick!" They both continued walking towards each other until they had met at a half-way point on the trail.

"Well?" asked Marianne hopefully.

"It goes against my better judgment," replied Ranger Frederick, "but I suppose if you're determined enough you'd just come back without my permission anyway."

Marianne smiled and nodded. "Yes, I suppose I would." she admitted softly.

"Alright then. I'll report that all campers have cleared for the season but you can guarantee I'll be up here checking on you and the boy by snowmobile on a regular basis." Ranger Frederick said sternly.

"That would actually be very much appreciated. Thank you so much," said Marianne with tears in her eyes.

Ranger Frederick said, "Damn it, Marianne my wife and I would be happy to put you up until you find another job."

"I know you would," said Marianne as a single tear streamed down her cheek. "Thank your wife for me but I refuse to accept charity if there's any other way I can manage." She turned to start back up the trail. "Oh, by the way, Fred, did my friend in London phone you?"

"That she did," he replied. "If there's any news regarding potential employment, she'll message me and you'd better believe I'll high tail it up here to collect you."

"Thanks, again!" called Marianne as she hiked back toward the camp site.

"God bless you and keep you, Marianne," Fred uttered under his breath. "God bless you."

Blood in the Sink

"Nina!" George hollered frantically as he ran through the house looking for his wife. "Nina!" he yelled again.

"Good heavens, George!" exclaimed Nina as she wiped her hands on a kitchen towel. "What is the matter?"

"Oh, Nina!" George said, still half shouting but completely winded. "I... I thought...," he could barely speak. He leaned against the wall to catch his breath.

"Come on, George," Nina said rather impatiently. "Your supper's ready." George followed Nina into the dining room and they sat down at the table together to eat. "How was your day, George?" Nina asked and began portioning food onto their plates. George gulped down an entire glass of water before he could answer.

Finally, he was able to ask, "Nina, why is the sink in the loo filled with blood? I saw that much blood and I thought..." George paused.

"You thought what, dear?" asked Nina.

"Well, I thought you must be, you know, dead," George stammered. Nina looked at him for a moment then began to cackle like a hen.

"Oh, George, you say the oddest things!" She continued

to laugh as she inserted a forkful of green beans into her mouth.

George did not share his wife's sense of humor on the matter. "Nina," he said, attempting to get her to focus on what he had to say. "Nina, why is there so much blood in the sink in the loo?"

"Really, George," Nina said, feeling quite annoyed, "Can't this topic wait until after supper?" George stared at his plate. He was confused and hungry.

"I suppose so," he said and cut into his slab of pot roast. The couple ate in relative silence.

After supper, they adjourned to the living room to watch a bit of telly and have a relaxing cup of tea. "Nina," George said as pleasantly as he could. "Will you now please tell me why there is so much blood in the sink in the loo?" Nina sipped her tea then gently set it to rest on the coffee table. For apparently no reason at all, she started to giggle. "What's the matter with you, woman?" George asked angrily.

"Well," giggled Nina, "I've never thought about this until just now but isn't it funny that we always set our tea on the coffee table. If we have coffee, it's always in the morning in the kitchen so we set our coffee on the table in there." George stared at her expressionlessly. She continued. "So we never set anything on the coffee table except tea!" She resumed giggling while George massaged his temples with his fingers. Nina kept right on.

"So why do we call it a coffee table and not a tea table? Or for that matter, why don't we call it a tea and biscuit table. Or perhaps a tea and biscuit table with a magazine section."

Nina probably would have kept right on talking and adding to the long list of items they should tack onto the phrase "tea table" if George hadn't stood up abruptly and roared, "NINA! I demand to know this instant why there is so much blood in the sink in the loo!"

Nina glared at George seriously. "George, if you get your blood pressure all up in the dangerous zone, I swear..."

George didn't have to interrupt her this time. She could tell by the look on his face she could stall him no longer. "George, I think you'd better sit down." George complied. "George," Nina said again as if she had to keep reminding him of his own name, "I've killed Eugene."

"Eugene from next door?" George asked with bewilderment.

"Yes," replied Nina. "Eugene from next door."

George slumped down in his overstuffed chair. "Eugene...," he said one more time. "Nina, why? Why Eugene?"

"I don't want to tell you. You'll be angry with me," said Nina as she fidgeted with her napkin. George appeared to be in a state of shock, or perhaps like he may be hoping this was a dumb joke and Eugene would jump up from behind the sofa and yell "Gotcha!" but that wasn't the case. He could tell by Nina's demeanor.

"Darling," said George, "I really feel I'm owed an explanation as to why you killed our next door neighbor." Nina sighed heavily.

"Of course you're owed an explanation," she said. "We were having an affair."

George squinted his eyes. "You and Eugene from next door were having an affair... and you killed him today."

"Yes, and yes." answered Nina. "I know you're probably really furious with me right now, George, but please don't shout. It's been a long day."

"Yes, I imagine it has been," said George. "Did you have sex with Eugene today, darling?"

"Yes," said Marianne, "But only a little."

"I'm just curious, darling," said George as he leaned forward to resume drinking his tea. "How does one have sex 'a little'?"

"You're being smart with me and I don't appreciate it," Nina huffed. "What I meant was that usually when I have sex with Eugene, we have it multiple times in one afternoon, or morning, whichever the case may be. Today we only had sex the one time."

"The time right before you killed him," said George.

"Yes," answered Nina.

"Is that why you killed him?" asked George. "Was it because he could only manage the one time today?"

"George, I have warned you about being smart with me. If you want to know what happened, you'll please keep a civil tongue in your head," snapped Nina.

"Yes, yes. You're right," apologized George. "It's just that when we took our vows those seventeen years ago, we made rules about this sort of thing."

"Don't you think I know that?" screeched Nina as she began to cry. "I've never broken the rules before and I'd think you could show me a bit of leniency. It's not like you never do anything wrong. Why, just yesterday you failed to put your soiled stockings in the hamper."

"A fairly minor offense, considering, don't you think?" quipped George.

"Yes," agreed Nina, "It's just that you're attacking me and I feel the need to lash out at you. There was that trip to New York that time when you...". George interrupted her before she could finish.

"Nina, that's not fair. We were so young back then it's like we didn't know any better. We didn't know how important the vows were." Nina sniffled into her napkin and nodded.

"Yes, I understand, George, but she was still in the hotel room right next to ours. To this day I wonder how many times that connecting door between the rooms was put to use while I was in the sauna."

George moved over onto the sofa next to Nina and put his arm around her. "You're right," he said. Youth really isn't an excuse. I, too, broke the rules but you must concede this is worse. I mean, our next door neighbor. How will we explain that, Nina?"

"We'll move. I'm sick of it here anyway. We'll just move," insisted Nina. It was a lot for George to take in all at once but he did know they would have to move away.

He rubbed his hand up and down Nina's back and asked "Darling, what did you do with Eugene's body?"

Nina had regained her composure and she sat up straight because she knew time was of the essence. "We had him for supper," she said.

George said, "I don't believe it. I just don't believe it. Never in the recesses of my deepest imagination did I ever think Eugene would be so tender and delicious."

"Yes, he really was quite, wasn't he?" asked Nina with a half smile. "Can you forgive me this one indiscretion, George?"

George pretended to think for a moment but he already

knew the answer. "Of course I will, darling. It's just imperative that you fully understand why we have the rule about not killing close to home."

"Oh, George, I do understand," said Nina as she caressed his hand. "I understand. It's just that, well, Eugene was not adventurous at all in bed and I tried to break it off with him several times but he just wouldn't listen. He kept coming over with that ridiculously small penis of his and..."

"Hush now, darling," George said as he gave his wife a squeeze. "Eugene was a Godawful bore and he never did return my socket wrench. It's not like you deprived the world of a great scientific mind or anything." George took in a deep breath and let it out slowly. "God, I hate moving," he said.

"So do I," agreed Nina. "Just this once couldn't we torch the whole place?" George mulled this prospect over.

"I don't see why not," he said. "It's not like we've made a pattern out of arson."

"Oh, George, I do love you so," said Nina and kissed him on the cheek.

"I love you too, darling, but you still didn't explain why the sink in the loo is full of blood."

Nina took a defensive position. "Well, I was going to make gravy but I ran out of time."

"You were going to make gravy in the sink in the loo?" George shuddered. "Nina, that's disgustingly unsanitary!"

"Well, sweetheart, I had vegetables in the kitchen sink and I was going to boil the gravy, for crying out loud. Besides. I keep a spotless bathroom! You try having an affair, killing the neighbor, forensically cleaning up the mess and having a home cooked meal on the table in a timely manner!"

"Calm down, Nina. It doesn't matter now. We've got a lot to do before sun up."

"Yes, we do, George, so stop taking jabs at me."

"I will, darling. I will stop," said George, "but I do have one last question."

"What is that dear?" asked Nina.

"We aren't going to get any diseases from Eugene are we? I mean, we really don't know that much about him."

"George, I'm utterly shocked you would ask such a question. You know I am steadfast about the use of condoms."

"I know that, Nina, it's just that supper, although delicious, was a little juicy. Are you sure you cooked him thoroughly?"

Nina jumped off the sofa as if she'd been bitten by

something from behind. "Now you're saying I don't know how to cook. Is that it?"

"Nina..." moaned George. "Just go get the petrol can."

"Certainly, dear. I'll bake a cake on my way to the garage as well as..."

Nina's voice trailed off into the distance. George finished his tea which was now stone cold. "I wish someone had told me how difficult marriage can be," George said to himself as he rolled up his sleeves. "It's going to be a very long night."

No, It Isn't Just the Wind

The Wessemann children, Todd and Lucy, had convinced their parents they were too old for a sitter and that they could manage on their own while Mum and Dad went to the office party. Mum and Dad finally gave in to the children on the condition that if they changed their minds, they would call Gina to come over. Gina was the kids' usual sitter. The kids agreed, Mum and Dad said their goodbyes and Todd and Lucy celebrated their independence by jumping up and down on all the furniture in Dad's "off limits" den.

When they tired of that, they each got a dish of ice cream and settled down to watch a movie. "Nothing too scary," Todd requested.

"I know," Lucy said with sarcasm, then whispered "bloody infant" to herself so Todd wouldn't hear. They agreed on a movie and it was shaping up to be a great night. "Do you hear that?" asked Lucy.

"Stop trying to scare me," wailed the infantile Todd.

"No, I'm serious. Listen," Lucy told him. There was a screeching sound coming from the kitchen. "It's probably just the wind," said Lucy and went back to watching the movie. Todd wasn't so certain.

"Um, Lucy? How does the wind make a scratchy sound

on the window?"

Lucy dragged Todd into the kitchen and showed him how near the tree grew to the window and explained that when the wind blew, the ends of the smaller branch screeched across the window. "Oh, okay," said Todd, satisfied with this simple explanation. The kids returned to the movie. An enormous bang came from somewhere upstairs. Todd nearly jumped out of his britches. "Was that the wind, too, Lucy?"

Lucy looked around the room and said, "Yeah, I'm sure it was just the wind." That's what she said, but Todd thought her eyes betrayed her. To him, Lucy looked scared. "Let's just watch the movie," said Lucy as she tried not to make eye contact with Todd.

A little while passed and Todd and Lucy had all but forgotten about the noises or even remembered they had been alarmed. "That was a good movie!" Todd announced.

"It was a chick flick and it was stupid," replied Lucy. With the telly off now, Lucy could once again hear the screeching noise coming from the kitchen.

"You said it was just the wind," Todd reminded her.

"I know," said Lucy as she stared into the kitchen.

Todd said, "This time I'll be the one to prove it to you!" He skipped to the living room window and peered out into the front yard. "Yep, Lucy, you were exactly right. It's the wind by the kitchen window." Lucy breathed a little sigh of relief.

Then Todd said, "That's a really neat trick!"

"What's a really neat trick?" asked Lucy.

"How the wind can blow by the kitchen window but not in the front yard! Boy, no wonder the weather guy has so much trouble with his forecasts. Gosh, when you're up against tricky stuff like that...".

"SHUT UP!" yelled Lucy, which nearly sent Todd into a seizure.

"What's wrong?" he whispered. Lucy looked out the front window. Todd was right. There wasn't so much as a slight breeze. The leaves on the trees in the front yard were perfectly still. So still, in fact, the yard looked very much like an oil painting. "What's wrong?" Todd whispered again. This time Lucy answered him.

"There is no wind. Not in the front, not in the back, not anywhere." Todd let loose with a blood curdling scream that would have scared even the most self-respecting apparition, burglar or kidnapper far, far away.

"CALL GINA!" screamed Todd. His entire body had gone rigid and his eyes were popped open bigger than she knew was possible.

"Alright!" yelled Lucy, "Just don't scream any more! Gina probably heard you down at her house!"

"I HOPE SHE DID!" shrieked Todd. "I HOPE SHE'S ALREADY ALMOST HERE!"

Despite being scared herself, Lucy thought at that precise moment she might be capable of handing Todd over to whatever lurked outside. She picked up the phone and called Gina on her mobile.

"Hey, Lucy!" Gina chimed happily. "How's everything going?"

"Well actually," Lucy began with a slightly trembling voice. "Todd's really scared and he wanted me to ask you to come over. We've heard some noises but I'm sure it's just the wind."

"What wind?" asked Gina. I'm out on the front porch having a ciggy and there's no wind at all."

Lucy swallowed hard. She already knew there was no wind. "Could you come over anyway, Gina? I'll tell my parents how scared Todd was and they'll pay you extra."

"Alright," said Gina, I'll see you in a couple minutes." Gina hung up her mobile. Lucy also hung up and assured Todd that Gina was on her way. Todd didn't answer. He was too busy staring out the kitchen window into the dark back yard. A white hazy figure floated up into the air. Then another, and still another. Todd and Lucy stood huddled together waiting for Gina the Magical Rescuer of

Frightened Children to ring the doorbell.

Gina leaned against the far side of the tree in the Wessemann's back yard. She decided she would allow herself one more cigarette before she went around to the front of the house and rang the bell. She watched her puffs of smoke waft up into the pitch black sky. She contemplated babysitting and how eventually all good things come to an end. All the kids in the neighborhood were getting older. All of them didn't frighten as easily as the Wessemann kids. Soon she'd have to get a real job. "Yeah, they better pay me extra," Gina said aloud. "I think I threw my back out shaking that damn tree." She took one last long drag from her cigarette, exhaled her final "apparition" and headed for the front door.